John R. Tait

Dolce far Niente

Anatiposi

John R. Tait

Dolce far Niente

Reprint of the original.

1st Edition 2023 | ISBN: 978-3-38230-830-8

Anatiposi Verlag is an imprint of Outlook Verlagsgesellschaft mbH.

Verlag (Publisher): Outlook Verlag GmbH, Zeilweg 44, 60439 Frankfurt, Deutschland
Vertretungsberechtigt (Authorized to represent): E. Roepke, Zeilweg 44, 60439 Frankfurt, Deutschland
Druck (Print): Books on Demand GmbH, In de Tarpen 42, 22848 Norderstedt, Deutschland

Dolce far Niente.

DOLCE FAR NIENTE.

BY

JOHN R. TAIT.

PHILADELPHIA:
PARRY AND McMILLAN.
1859.

CONTENTS.

1*

vi   CONTENTS.

DEDICATORY SONNET.

TO THOMAS BUCHANAN READ.

Do you remember how that once, from Rome,
  I sent you a poor wild-flower? tribute small
  To thy great kindness! yet upon the wall
It grew, where bends the blue aërial dome
Above the Coloseum; and the loam
  That gave it life was sacred; and o'er all
  Reigned present the grand Past imperial!
And you disdained not the poor scentless bloom.
Thus may it be with these poor songs of mine—
  Less mine than Italy's, born of her skies,
Rocked to the rhythm of the swaying vine,
  And nurtured where all night the rose replies
In perfumed whisperings, while all the vale
Rings with the joy of the enamored nightingale.

CINCINNATI, August 30, 1858.

DOLCE FAR NIENTE.

DOLCE FAR NIENTE.

THE wind among these agéd cypress trees
   Drowsily whispereth a dreamy tale;
And the far city's hum, like that of bees,
   Floats faintly to me down the misty vale.
Even this aërial arch of blue intense
Peoples with dreams my sleepy indolence.

The sluggard river slowly creeps along
   As if aweary of its onward race,
And seems to murmur a complaining song—
   A lingering farewell to its native place

In the deep passes of the Apennines,
Where winds and twilight dwell among the pines.

The sunlight sleeps upon the waters now,
    Which sleep themselves, scarce rippling in the sun;
The weary laborer leaves the lagging plough
    Half-way within the furrow last begun,
And throws himself upon a grassy mound,
Where a cool shadow falls athwart the ground.

Each tender blossom droops its tinted cheek,
    O'erweighed with odor that around it lives—
As a young maiden's heart grows faint and weak
    With the sweet burthen of the love it gives;
And tremulous they sigh in bashful bliss
As if a-dreaming of the south wind's kiss.

No living thing is near me to destroy
    The airy fabrics that my fancy rears,
Save the sweet bee, who, with melodious joy,
    From bud to bloom all luscious-laden steers;
And e'en the bright-eyed lizard 'neath the spray,
In silent slumber lies all coiled away.

I feel like one, who, drunk with charméd wine,
    Cares naught for other joys that Heaven bestows—
Fame, wealth, love, power, e'en poesy divine,
    To me what are they, in this rapt repose,
But idle visions of a fevered brain,
The which to miss, not have, seems greatest gain?

O luxury divine!   Come, Ceres! spread
    A slumberous couch of poppy-fringéd sheaves!
Come, laughing Bacchus! from the boughs o'erhead
    Rain down a drapery of rustling leaves—
While Proserpine shakes all her Lethean flowers,
With perfume leading me to dreamland bowers.

Field, hill and sky grow dim—not vain the prayer—
    My willing eyelids dissipate the day,
A lotus influence rocks my soul in air—
    Far, far beyond, the world is veiled away.
O Ceres, Bacchus, Proserpine—fair three!
Is this the land of Dreams, or Italy?

THE FAIR IN THE PIAZZA.

I.

ONCE at Florence, near the Duomo,
   In the soft Italian air,
On the ground were spread around me
   The piled treasures of a Fair,
With the Contadini merchants,
   From the far Campagna skies;
Bearing to the shaded city
   All its sunshine in their eyes.

II.

Here the pretty Tuscan maidens,
   With their night of falling hair,
And their careless liquid laughter,
   Made rich music through the Square.
There, a wild Etrurian shepherd,
   Piping some soft pastoral tune,

'Till I saw the fleecy hill-sides
   Whitening 'neath a harvest moon.

III.

By my side there walked a Poet,
   One whom love would fondly name,
But her silvery praise is drownéd
   In the wider breath of Fame.
And we dreamed, and talked together,
   Speaking only of our dreams,
As each novelty around us
   Gave an impulse to the themes.

IV.

There were old-time arms and armor,
   Rough with scars from Palestine,
And rich goblets, dry and dusty,
   Where once sparkled Chian wine.
There were pictures, dark and ragged,
   Of dim saints and virgins mild;
And a hundred bas'-relievi
   Of the mother and the child:—

2

V.

Robbings of old ruined convents
   In the vales of Apennines;
Or, perchance, of nearer churches,
   And neglected household shrines;—
There were books, decayed and dusty,
   Of the old monastic ages;
And like monks within a cloister,
   Slept the worms amid their pages.

VI.

Rare illuminated missals
   Made a melancholy show
Of the melodies majestic
   Of two hundred years ago,
Now unchanted in the churches,
   Though, if life's dim veil were riven,
One might hear their solemn music
   In the choral courts of heaven.

VII.

There were lutes which oft had echoed
   Songs of chivalry and war,

And the gentler amorous roundel
 Of the wandering troubadour;
Stringless now, where once fair fingers
 Cast a shadow from the moon—
Hands now dust; but still the shadow
 Seemed to play a mournful tune.

VIII.

One of these—it was a broken,
 Quaintly carved old instrument,
Costly, inlaid with the rarest
 Woods, with gems and pearls besprent;
While across the ivory bridge, and
 Sighing to the evening breeze,
Seven silver chords were swaying
 From the delicate pearl keys.

IX.

When my friend saw, smiling sadly,
 Said he: "How much strange romance
Could yon ruined plaything tell us,
 If awakened from its trance;

Oh, how much of tenderest story,
   Plaintive melodies of tears,
And what gusts of joy have thrilled it
   In its history of years!

X.

"Think you if those riven chords were
   Strung again as at their birth,
They would melt to modern music,
   And respond to modern mirth?
Or would not the night-wind's fingers,
   Floating freely o'er the strings,
Wake a dirge for times forgotten,
   And a sigh for vanished things?"

XI.

Lightly laughing at his sadness,
   Which my own heart also knew,
"By the ghost of Saint Cecilia,
   And by all the minstrel crew!"
Cried I, "it were well to prove it,
   Although, like Italia dead,

Much I fear 'tis but the poor shell
   Whence the poet-soul has fled!"

XII.

So I bought it for a trifle,
   Scarcely more than once was thrown
To some mediæval minstrel
   When its fortunes were his own:
But to me it is a treasure
   Kings might strive to buy in vain;
For it whispers me such tales I know
   Its soul is back again.

2*

LAURA.

Fair moon! that witnessed my delight,
    As—Laura's little hand in mine—
We walked, the cloudless summer night,
    Beneath the purple-clustered vine,
Say, hast e'er fanned a fairer face
    With the mild splendor of thy wing,
Or known a form of gentler grace
    Than hers of whom I fondly sing?

Ye stars! that in her happy eyes
    Looked down and saw yourselves more bright,
Speak! have you ever, from the skies,
    Beheld a being half so light?
Was Eve more lovely when, new born,
    The fairest thing in Paradise,
The world's first lover woke at morn,
    She flashed on his astonished eyes?

Ye trees, whose branches o'er my head
 Waved pendulous that blessed eve,
And heard the loving vows she said,
 Do love-birds sweeter strains e'er weave?
Or do the tales the soft winds bring,
 Which make thy whispering leaves rejoice;
Or silvery streamlets murmuring
 In melody surpass her voice?

O sea! that kissed our feet that night,
 Did heavenly Venus fairer roam,
When like the Iris, clothed in light,
 She leapt to life amid thy foam;
Or when thy waves bore from the land
 Egypt's dark queen, had she more charms—
Or Hero, when upon the strand
 She clasped Leander in her arms?

Winds! that bore from the garden's bloom,
 Like spirits of the loved in death,
The soul of flowers, a sweet perfume,
 Say, was it sweeter than her breath?

And when you kissed her blushing cheek,
    And nestled in her auburn hair,
And sinuous, stirred her bosom meek,
    Didst thou not seek a warm death there?

They all are silent—moon and stars,
    And trees, and ever-rolling sea,
And winds that, yoked to fairy cars,
    Bear endless freights of melody—
They speak not; yet, O loving heart!
    What boots it what the answer be;
Though the whole world deny each part,
    Is she not more than all to thee?

ALL.

A WREATH and a wedding-ring,
 A home in his heart and hall,
A snow-white palfrey on which to ride,
And the happy life of the happiest bride,
 All this he promised me—all!

My love and my purity,
 A heart free from sinful thrall,
My cheerful home in the flowery vale,
And the roses that bloomed where my cheek is pale,
 All this I gave to him—all!

Laughter and bitter scorn,
 And tears that blind ere they fall,
A wicked breast and a wildered mind,
And a conscience that trembles in every wind,
 All this he has given me—all!

An early and nameless grave,
　　Obscure by the churchyard wall,
Where, though they drink in no pitying tear,
The flowers like me may fall withered each year,
　　Is all I can pray for—all!

EACH FLOWER THAT BLOOMS AT EVENING.

EACH flower that blooms at evening
    Is the child of morning dews,
And the reaper only gathers,
    In the harvest, what he strews.
Thus memory moulds the poet—
    The past is the only muse!

This I feel in looking backward
    To the days when I was young;
Mute I gaze upon the desert,
    Where but scanty flowers belong;
And my heart would soar in singing,
    But, alas! it knows no song.

Born and bred within a city
    And the stifled air of schools,
Nature rather fled than wooed me
    When they led me to her rules,

Forcing me to view her teachings
    Through the philosophic fools.

Even the mysteries of heaven,
    And the stars' illusive store,
Did they cheat me of, exchanging
    For their astronomic lore;
And the bright round earth they gave me
    Geologic dust—no more!

Fame a phantom, love a folly,
    Was the story often told;
Fancy, feeling, and affection,
    Things to purchase and be sold;
And that really true ambition
    Pointed to a goal of gold.

Thus I grew amid the teachings
    Of the economic throng,
And they uttered them so kindly
    That I could not deem them wrong.
Need I wonder, in my sadness,
    That my heart now knows no song?

THE DEAD BIRD.

WALKED I with a widowed husband
   By the Sercio's classic stream,
Where the chestnut's verdant branches
   Cooled the noontide's sultry beam.

Light we spoke and light we jested,
   And we laughed, but never smiled—
Heartache often is to laughter
   Parent of the wayward child!

When the moon, that last night wandered,
   Wan and wasted, o'er the sky,
Entered with the month—her infant,
   He had watched his infant die.

And, as when the month departing,
   Its pale parent fades and dies,

3

Thus the mother, broken-hearted,
　　Sought her child in other skies.

And the day itself was solemn—
　　Sleep is kindred unto Death—
And o'er all the dreaming landscape
　　Summer seemed to hold her breath.

By the mill the scanty waters
　　Rippled o'er the stony ground;
And the stately mill-wheel slowly
　　Told the minutes in its round.

Nothing else of sound was near us
　　Save the wind's low mournful moan,
And from out the locust's branches
　　The cicala's monotone.

And our speech was hushed in sadness,
　　And our eyes lay on the ground,
Walking 'mid the ferns and rushes,
　　Where a birdling corpse we found.

How it happened, now, I know not—
    But he touched it with his staff,
And—O Christ! how wild his eyes were,
    And how fearful was his laugh!

And the thing—the slimy, crawling,
    Dreadful lesson of decay—
Oh! I never can forget it,
    Though I live to Judgment-Day!

And I gazed in fear and horror,
    Till I heard his long-drawn breath;
And then turning, saw the question
    In his eyes—God! is this Death!

His pale look was turned to heaven,
    Where the white clouds moveless hung,
Like the smoke of viewless censers,
    Through the vault by angels swung;—

When, from out the branches near us,
    Slowly rose a wingéd pair—

Birds they were, yet seemed like seraphs,
   Springing upwards through the air.

Higher, higher, until they vanished,
   In the clouds they left beneath;
When I seemed to hear a voice say—
   Husband—Father—this is Death!

SPRING IN ITALY.

I.

WHEN first she left—fair Proserpine—
  Her dark connubial bowers,
She quaffed a cup of Lethe's wine,
  And breathed upon the flowers:—
And hence the influence so divine,
  That freights the spring-tide hours.

II.

The violet hides by sleepy streams;
  The bee nods o'er the clover;
Between the corn the poppy gleams,
  Where opiate odors hover;
The lily like a maiden seems,
  A-dreaming of a lover.

3*

III.

In sighs the faint airs swoon along
    The margin of the river;
Enamored of the South, their song
    Breathes of its softness ever;
And dying, still the notes prolong
    Till all the aspens quiver.

IV.

My soul is in the deep blue skies,
    And careless who approve me;
I lie, and watch with half-shut eyes,
    The clouds sail by above me;
And see in each the visions rise
    Of distant friends who love me.

V.

Oh, deem them not—the moments—lost,
    Thus passed in dreamy bowers;
Our lives are like rude rocks, enmossed
    By spring-time sun and showers;
And men who God forget, life-tossed,
    Adore the tranquil hours.

VI.

There are many lessons that the heart
   Can never learn in labor;—
Too much of constant use will hurt
   The edge of keenest sabre;
And he who farthest holds the mart,
   Lives nearest to his neighbor.

VII.

Oh! there is love amid the woods,
   And goodness in the gloaming,
And naught of evil e'er intrudes
   Upon the heart here coming;
While care soon flies the solitudes,
   Where only bees are humming.

VIII.

All nature blooms in beauty round;
   The soul is the receiver,
And grateful from the grassy ground,
   Leaps up to thank the Giver:—
Joys lost with Eden it hath found,
   To hallow it forever.

SONG FOR A SUMMER AFTERNOON.

I.

MIDSUMMER reigns over land and sea—
The season of love and passion and glee,
Summer, that like a maiden destraye,
First crowns herself with blossoms gay,
Then tramples the blooms in the dusty way.
Summer, the child of a tropical sun,
And the parent of joy since her life begun;
Cradled upon the swaying palm,
And fed on the purple lotus leaves
And spices and poppy's milk of balm,
Until her very breath receives
The opiate influence, and she gives
To the airs she stirs with her passing wing,
A similar influence maddening.

II.

East and West, and North and South,
She breathes upon with her rosy mouth,
Over the rustling fields of grain;
Over the desert, over the main;
Over the mountain and over the plain;
Through dim avenues of woods,
And down in the valleys' solitudes;
All nature greets her joyous reign;
Through all the wide world up and down,
The laureate birds pursue her train;
The mountain doffs his icy crown,
And even ocean forgets to frown;—
And I—oh, I love her, and welcome with glee
Fair Summer—the empress of land and sea!

WRITTEN AT BELLOSGUARDA.

I.

I'VE been reading your beautiful letter,
   And I sit in the day's decline,
In the light where the shadow has left me,
   Since the sun has glode west of the pine;
Till my soul on thy love-words uplifted,
   As on heavenward wings, is blest,
And in dreams, like my form is enfolded
   In the roseate hues of the west.

II.

Below me the city is dreaming,
   Like a nun in the twilight of prayer,
With one dome flaming golden to Heaven—
   A glorified forehead in air!
While the moon slowly rising in beauty,
   Her light from Fiesole flings,

And o'er all smiles a placid approval
  Like an angel on luminous wings.

III.

On the breeze harvest odors are mingled
  With the breath of innumerous flowers;
And cicala's monotonous whirring,
  With the music of vesper-voiced towers;
While from yon cypress alley, illumined
  By the lucciola's timorous fires
As a chapel with tapers, the anthem
  Is commencing of nightingale choirs.

IV.

All is beautiful here, yet my fond heart
  Deems this alien landscape ideal,
And constant to home and to thee, love!
  In the Past recognizes the Real:
Till again as in summers departed,
  Sit I reading the tales in your eyes;
Or tracing your thought's gentle current,
  Ere it rippled to speech, by your sighs.

V.

Looking westward, far into the cloud-land,
 I renew all the visions of years,
All the dreams which we dreamed of together,
 All the gladness of youth—all its tears;—
And the while, as each vision departing,
 Memory weaves a half sorrowful spell,
My soul in its sadness grows stronger—
 Hope brightening at every farewell.

VI.

Thus I dream, sitting here with your letter,
 While the light slowly creeps up the pine,
Resting now on its top, like a seraph
 Just unfolding his pinions divine:—
It is gone! and the gloom is descending,
 But the light your remembrance has given,
Shall endure when the sun now but passing,
 Shall have vanished forever from heaven.

THE SIRENS.

It is said when the sirens died
  They sang a wild farewell,
So sweet and sad that the echoes replied
  From each gusty citadel:
And all the inhabitants of the sea,
All living things in the waves that be—
Dolphin and shark and leviathan,
The mermaid and the bluff merman,
And all the sea-birds in the air
Gathered to listen, and hear despair.
And the winds, enamored of the strain,
Bore it afar o'er the sleeping main,
To the ears of a sailor from Hindoostan,
As he stood at the helm of an Indiaman;
And he maddened with joy and leaped into the sea,
And his barque was lost on a rocky lee.

4

II.

A merchant heard it in his dream,
　And muttered with prayerful lips,
For to him it seemed as a mariner's scream,
　And he thought of his freighted ships;
And a monk who bore the sacred Host
To a dying fisherman on the coast,
Saw the billows, like crimson waves of hell,
Leap to the lighthouse pinnacle,
And drown the beacon, what time the glare
Of corpse-fires burned through the sultry air:
And the sailor's wife dreamed of a dripping shroud,
And awoke to find the storm was loud;
For the song was ended, the sirens gone,
And the uncontrollable waves leaped on.

III.

And ever since when, wailing ghosts,
　Fled into the night those sisters three,
And leaped from the earth's forsaken coasts
　Into the ocean eternity,
The mariner lists, with incredulous smile,
To the legend of the sirens' isle,

And laughs at the song; yet often he hears
It shouted into his drowning ears
By spirit voices; and still the shells,
In their purple and pink and pearly cells,
Retain the echoes, that seem as the roar
Of disconsolate waves on a desert shore.
But in truth they are the words of that wizard dirge,
Which, if man could understand, would urge
The brain to madness by the excess
Of the legend's exceeding loveliness.

THE DILIGENCE.

I.

ALL day the rain
On each grimy pane
Bleared monotonous drops and lines
Across the square-foot of misty hill,
And foreground of drenched, forsaken vines,
That I stared inanely at until
The solitude seemed a numbing pain,
Frozen on my heart and brain.

II.

'Twas ever the same
In that dismal frame,
The forms might change, but never the gloom.
Now a long line of olives, gnarled and pale,
Gibbered like ghosts, as we passed; like a tomb
Seemed each cot, so silent and cold in the vale;

Each finger-board swung like a corpse in a chain,
And the weariness froze in my heart and brain.

III.

Now down a street
Clattered the feet
Of the steaming horses, until at the door
Of the beggarly inn we would stop, when the palms
Of a pauper mob, with a whine to implore,
And a curse or a prayer to reward the alms,
Would dispute with the rain at the grimy pane,
And the misery froze in my heart and brain.

IV.

Then a curse and a crash,
A rumble and splash,
The articulate tread of each hoof, and again
A bare wall or two; then the olives and vines,
All the desolate landscape, the mist and the rain,
And the brown rugged peaks of the dim Apennines,
Ridged and black as the forehead of Cain,
And the frozen sadness in heart and brain.

4*

V.

See! down to the right,
The sea, black as night,
And afar in the haze looms a ship like a dream—
A nightmare still—for the winds, like sleep,
Are folded in silence and motionless seem:
And still down the pane the raindrops creep,
The solitude seems a numbing pain,
And the loneliness crushes my heart and brain.

VILLA D'ESTE.

A PALACE garden in a golden clime,
Long walks obscured by odorous shadows thrown
From old ancestral pines and myrtle trees,
And stainéd marbles draped with clinging vines;
Green beds of grasses and sweet violets;
Quaint mediæval parterres; girandoles,
Who have long forgot their watery fantasies,
Dribbling their feeble tears into the pool
The goldfish haunt no more.   Arion there
Still rides the dolphin, but his harp is gone;
And hushed the gushing laughter of the nymphs,
Still flying from the Triton's vain pursuit.

Amid the laurel of a tangled brake
Gleams hornéd Pan, and a fair, headless form—
'Twas Bacchus once—the cluster-crownéd head
Lies prone amid the grasses at his feet.

A ruined bower still affects to hide
Coy Venus in its amorous retreat;
Astonished lizards flash across her breast,
And dart a timorous glance around her neck,
And vanish with a rustle in the leaves.
Here is a seat, now flecked with humid stains—
Green and unwholesome white and splash of brown—
Whereon once lovers whispered in the shade.

Out in the sunshine, where twin lions guard
The marble stairway, sits and sings a child—
A seven-years' darling with great lustrous eyes,
Sitting alone, and twining, as she sings,
A garland of bright flowers, with which she decks
The lion's brows, like Una—then her laugh
Fills all the alleys with its joyous thrill.

A VIOLET FOUND AT ARQUA.

A WEEK ago I pressed unto my lips
The earliest violet, by fair finger tips
Gathered ere the inquisitive bee had found
Its honeyed chalice peeping from the ground;
Before the passionate wooing of the sun
Had kissed away the dainty tear that shone
In its mild eye, for there was only one.
Itself an azure dewdrop did it seem,
Which the young April, starting from his dream,
Had shook upon the grass from off his wing,
While all his larks went heralding the spring.
I see before me now the healthful dawn,
The sun's rays slanting o'er the dewy lawn,
The sharpened purple of the Ægean hills,
Above the misty rivers and the rills;
The nearer woodlands all aglow with fires
Ethereal, which the far-off village spires

And cottage windows flame back at the sun;
The ploughman in the fields, their toil begun—
Toil that is pleasure in the beamy morn,
And wealth accomplished in the future corn.
And then the maiden at whose side I pressed
(Each fondly emulous in the floral quest)—
How can I paint a loveliness so blest!
Her cheeks aflush with happiness and health,
And o'er her white neck prodigal the wealth
Of flashing ringlets flowed; her glad surprise
Deepening her dimples, sparkling in her eyes,
Her joyous laughter as the flower she found,
A gushing ripple of clear silver sound;
Her coy refusals when I asked it of her
With all the fond beseechings of a lover—
Beseechings fondly answered, for, now mine,
It blooms beside the love in Petrarch's book divine.

THE DAY-DREAM.

COMES back to me a dream long gone—
    A summer's day-dream 'mid the flowers
Bordering the formal verdure of the lawn,
    The mediæval parterres, and the bowers,
Rose-curtained like the dawn,

In the old ducal palace-grounds
    In Tivoli—(who has not heard
The story of the Duchess?   In the bounds
    Of Italy no fairer lady stirred,
No stranger tale resounds!)

I strode through the deserted halls,
    With the echoing silence half afraid,
And read the frescoed stories on the walls,
    And, leaning from the ivied balustrade,
Heard the far river's falls.

And listened, ere the light 'gan pale,
   To the sweet prattling of my guide,
A little red-lipped maiden, slight and frail,
   With great black eyes, that burned as she replied,
And gave the ancestral tale.

Her story, liquid as a song,
   Of ladies fair and knights in iron mail,
I heard not, though I listened, for among
   Its images yours shone, like Egypt's sail
Amidst the Roman throng.

When she had ceased, I sought the shade
   Of the tall Roman pines, which threw
Their pictured forms across a little glade
   Where hyacinths and choice exotics grew,
And the great fountains played.

Let those who can, tell by what art
   Our thoughts their form and color take;
Explain how secret sympathies will start,
   And how association seeks to make
Intelligible the heart:

Whence comes our love of images;
  What prompts the mind in quiet hours
To seek companionship in brooks and trees,
  And find similitudes in stars and flowers,
And voices in the breeze?

Let such as these tell why that dream
  Of you came o'er me in that vale,
Bearing my thought far from the plashing stream,
  The palace garden, and the antique tale,
Unless it is you seem

In one form to unite its bowers
  Of loveliness: thy voice combines
The music of its birds and fountain showers,
  Thine air as stately as its graceful pines,
And laughing as its flowers.

Thy nature's light and shade, imprest
  In alternating joy and sadness
Upon thy brow, more beauteous thus carest,
  As twilight shades to dreamier loveliness
The splendor in the west.

  5

TO A PAIR OF LAND BIRDS

THAT FLEW ON BOARD SHIP WHEN OUT AT SEA.

Poor trembling strangers, that the pirate breeze
 Hath rapt so far from the invisible shore,
And cast disconsolate on unpitying seas,
 Your wood-notes drowned amid the watery roar:

Bright argosies of song, like fairy wrecks
 Wailing unto the stars on coasts forlorn,
So wells your alien plaint upon our decks,
 Children of land! in leafy forests born.

Yet hail and welcome! for to me ye are
 Dear messengers from my dear native hills;
Your song a voice of welcome from afar—
 · A music full of memories of rills.

Here fold your wings! my heart has caught your
    rhyme,
    And aches to hear its anxious tenderness;
Sad are your voices, for in woods sublime
    Your nest laments ye in shrill plaintiveness.

Or do thy poet hearts regret old haunts
    'Mid flowers, and harvest fields, and slumberous
      bowers,
Where now brown autumn, like a conqueror, flaunts
    His crimson banners from the woodland towers?

I, too, have wandered from my forest home,
    Blown on the inexorable winds of Fate—
The sport, like ye, of storms and blinding foam,
    Like ye aweary, sad, and desolate.

Yet happy I, if to the fainting heart
    Of some lone mariner, on life's ocean tost,
My songs might bring the peace that yours impart,
    And wing its thoughts to some celestial coast.

But westward ho! my wanderings are o'er;
   Our brave prow cleaves the azure like a brand,
Flashing through ether; and behold! the shore—
   And hark! the topman's cry, "Land O! O, land!"

Adieu! across the sunset's amethyst
   The purple headlands widen o'er the blue;
And like twin stars, far in the golden mist,
   Your white wings beckon where my thoughts pur-
     sue!

MEETING.

I.

I HAD taken the near pathway,
　　Through the meadow's silent realm,
While the sunset glowed with memories
　　That no night could overwhelm;
When a-sudden flamed her casement
　　Through the old familiar elm.

II.

Yet I walked reluctant, trembling—
　　Trembling to my very knees—
And I stopped—"How bright the sunset
　　Burns amid the leafless trees,
And how odorous o'er the broom-corn
　　Comes the gentle evening breeze!"—

5*

III.

Said I to myself, unconscious,
　　Striving to ignore my fears,
And to stifle the deep yearning
　　That I knew would burst to tears;
For I felt all the tumultuous
　　Passion I had nursed for years.

IV.

Years of toil, of alien wandering
　　In far lands across the sea,
Lands where Tasso wept, and Petrarch
　　Loved in birdlike poesy—
Lands of poets and of lovers:
　　Now what were they all to me!

V.

All the long years seemed to vanish
　　As impalpable as dreams,
And I thought but of our parting,
　　Of her lips, her eyes—"It seems,"
Murmured I, "but yester morning—
　　Ah! the sun, how bright it beams!"

VI.

Then I gazed at all the windows,
    Drawing slowly near, until
Suddenly the door swum open,
    And a form passed o'er the sill,
Bounding down the steps, the pathway—
    Oh, my eager heart, be still!

VII.

There's a rose-tree in the garden,
    Of itself a summer bower,
And beside its sweet concealment,
    Mute I clasped my lovelier flower—
Oh, my rose-tree, bloom forever
    To the memory of that hour!

OVER DESOLATE MEADOW AND WOODLAND.

OVER desolate meadow and woodland
   Night broods on vast pinions of gloom—
All the rose-trees are wailing their flowers,
   All the violets asleep in their tomb;
And like Niobe out of the branches
   Pale Winter stares into my room.

Out of doors it is shivery and lonely,
   Neither moon nor stars are there;
And the wind, like a maiden forsaken,
   Goes murmuring her despair;
While the snow-flakes, like froth from her pale lips,
   Are blown on the blustering air.

All the fountains are frozen to silence,
   All the birds that once warbled have gone,

E'en the populous eaves are all songless,
   And the voluble nests in the lawn;
And the cock that gave warning of midnight
   Is muffled in silence till dawn.

Yet I care not for night nor for storm-wind,
   For my heart has a jubilant glow;
Its gardens of roses and violets
   Laugh derision at winter and snow;
And the song that it sings has a music
   The nightingale never can know.

For my love, my affectionate darling,
   As she kissed me a bashful good-night,
Told a tale her dear lips did not utter,
   Did she think I'd not read it aright?
Let the dark and the storm rule without, then,
   For within is a summer of light.

THE TWENTY SECOND OF FEBRUARY.

I.

Was there no sign in the frosty air,
   No portent in the winter sky,
To teach the tyrant's soul despair,
   And, like the flaming prophecy
Belshazzar saw on the palace wall,
   To threaten humanity's ancient lie,
And bid the thrones of monarchs fall?

II.

Was there no star in the Orient
   Beckoning Hope to the future West—
No visions with angelic melodies blent,
   No splendor illumining the rest
And the sad unrest of the captive's cell,
   To bid his heavy heart, opprest,
Rejoice with a joy invincible?

III.

Was there not this when he was born—
 Freedom's Messiah ? herald bright,
The aster of a nation's morn !
 The snows on Alleghenies' height
Flushed with red joy that dawn, the pines
 Bowed low and listened with delight,
And heard the story from the winds.

IV.

The solemn West, unpeopled, vast,
 In twilight solitudes lay still;
The rivers told it as they passed,
 Surging on slumberous shores; each hill
Rocked jubilant with echoings,
 Repeated o'er and o'er, until
The eagle heard them on sunward wings.

V.

Oh, Nature, thus does sympathy
 Feel your glad greeting of that morn !
The conscious prairies laughed with glee,
 Prophetic of the future corn;

The rivers dreamed of flashing keels,
  Of snow-winged navies forest born,
And thunders of innumerous wheels.

VI.

The rest is history's : but still
  Exultant in a nation's heart
The echo lives, which yet may fill
  The world with answers, that no art
Of courts may stifle ; whose glad boom
  Shall wake the astonished kings, and start
The avalanches of their doom.

MADELINE.

I.

LIGHT-HEARTED darling! Madeline,
Seated with your hand in mine,
Watching the river in its flow,
Dreamily rolling on far below,
Where, above, the locusts, lightly blown,
Snowed their odorous blossoms down,
And the rustling winds in the walnut tall
Made a drowsy lull like a waterfall,
And the leaves of the maple in the sun
Shivered to silver every one;
There where we sate 'neath the pendulous leaves,
That bent above us like vernal eaves,
No prince on his throne could prouder be
Than I—no princess compare with thee!

6

II.

Little Madeline, there was a word
Unuttered, yet its music stirred
My rapturous soul, as the voiceless breeze
Stirred every spray of the sensitive trees.
You crowned me with a wreath of green
Oak leaves, while your beauty crowned you queen.
And we talked of all irrelevant things,
Of the heartless world, and imaginings
Of future glory and goodness, and all
Save the one deep thought we dared not call
To our lips: and the wind still stirred the leaves,
And the birds sang out of the tuneful eaves;
Yet I was mute, save in telltale sighs,
And thou—but with most eloquent eyes.

TO ———.

But yesterday, amid the autumnal leaves
   My feet made echoes, in the rude path lying,
And on the lawn, where, when the summer's sheaves
   Were yet unbound, we walked, my heart then vieing
In joy with that the birds around the eaves
   Made voluble, joy that, too early dying,
Left me forlorn, for thou art gone—alone
I wander where Hope's withered leaves are strewn.

I gazed upon the landscape, bleak and brown,
   The lane, and all familiar things—the seat
On which we sate, the road that leads to town,
   The bare hills glooming through a mist's retreat,
From whose dim caves the rain stalked sullen down,
   Trampling the leaves with its innumerous feet;
And in my heart the falling rain of tears
Blurred Hope's fair vision with a mist of fears.

And when the eve had prematurely drawn
    The curtains, and we clustered round the fire,
Which lightened all our faces, on the lawn
    I heard the wet feet of the storm, while like a lyre
Tuned to a dirge, the wind sobbed, "She is gone!"
    Echoing my thought.   The laugh and song rose
      higher,
And merry voices whispered; yet for all
I missed one form, one shadow on the wall.

I murmured, "On my heart the shadow lies!"
    And thought of the fair form and features dear,
And memories of low-spoken words, replies
    Sweeter than music to the listening ear,
A dream of smiling lips and eloquent eyes,
    A snowy hand, a word unsaid, a tear,
A parting—and the shadow closer crept
Around my spirit, and I inly wept.

DOWN ON THE QUAY.

I.

Down on the quay the busy workmen
   Are toiling patiently and slow,
Like ants behind unwieldy burthens,
   Heaping, with many a stout "yeave-ho!"
The bales that rise, like mimic mountains
   In the spring-time, flecked with snow.

II.

Down on the quay I am sitting, thinking,
   Watching their toil with dreamy eyes,
And listening to the sea, that breaks
   On the shore, like a human heart, in sighs;
And the sights grow dim, and the sounds are hushed,
   And distant visions before me rise.

III.

Down on the quay the Orient pours
 Rare wealth of gems with a lavish hand,
And I seem, through them, to see the palms
 Nodding their plumes in that antique land,
And the weary caravan, winding slow
 O'er the desert from distant Samarcand.

IV.

Down on the quay the fluent Rhine
 Speaks in her wines.   The eloquent breeze
Whispers in odors of spice-isles afar,
 And pearl and coral fisheries,
And fabrics of wonderous looms, that come
 From fabulous lands across the seas.

V.

Down on the quay the ships have vanished,
 And the distant sea, so calm and blue,
And I see the tall magnolia, blooming
 On the sedgy banks of a still bayou,
And broad cotton-fields in the sunlight lying,
 Opening their creamy pods to view.

VI.

And the sultry air bears no pleasant voices,
   No perfume of happy harvest song,
Such as greet the morn in northern fields,
   Where freemen's throats the strains prolong;
But the sullen blow and the stifled moan
   Are the sounds which steal from the driven throng.

VII.

Down on the quay the fields have vanished,
   And I see a foreign factory rise,
And hear the multitudinous wheels
   Insult with their whirl the peaceful skies,
And over the din and the trouble of toil
   Hark to the laborer's weary sighs!

VIII.

Down on the quay the emigrant ship,
   With its freight of weary human hearts,
Tells many a tale of grief and want,
   Of poverty's woes and oppression's smarts—
Of famine that stalks amid fields of corn,
   And men who starve in crowded marts.

IX.

Down on the quay the glorious Past
   Rushes upon me.   I seem to see,
As the stars once saw on a night sublime,
   The indignant band, and the scattered tea,
Sown broadcast over the fertile waves—
   The seed of the harvest that made us free.

X.

Down on the quay the distant gun
   Of the home-bound steamer has summoned a crowd
Of anxious and hopeful hearts, where oft
   A nation has watched with pale lips as the loud
Low ominous thunder boomed over the waves,
   Till Freedom's bright lightning illumined the cloud.

XI.

Down on the quay the Future rears
   More glorious visions.   Trade's wingéd rod,
Wreathed no more with caduceus serpents, shall wave,
   And giant ships to the world abroad
Shall go—not freighted with sulphurous guns,
   But the light of Peace and the love of God.

XII.

Down on the quay the electric spark,
    Like a messenger dove, on luminous wings,
Shall speed the inevitable glorious news,
    Until with its joy the whole earth rings,
When again, as of old, shall be read the doom,
    In letters of flame, of the fallen kings.

THE TWO MEMNONS.

I.

I STOOD beside a statue on the plain
  Near Egypt's dusky pile,
What time the East, first conscious of the dawn,
  Flushed o'er the silent Nile.

All hushed and solemn lay the landscape wide,
  As one who lonely grieves;
The air so motionless it scarcely stirred
  The palm's light, pendulous leaves.

Within the garden, where the priests had wrought,
  'Neath the mysterious moon,
I saw the closed buds opening silently,
  As in a field of June.

At first they hung upon their tender stalks
    With dewy, blinking eyes,
In which the dreams still lingered; then I heard
    Low-breathed mysterious sighs.

And with a sudden splendor through the East
    The full-blown morning came,
And o'er the desert's golden waste the sun
    Wheeled his broad disk of flame.

Then, when the slanting beams had scarcely thrown
    The last star in eclipse,
Again I heard that low and marvellous tune
    Breathed through its marble lips.

An intermingling of all pleasant sounds
    Of earth, and sky, and sea—
Full of exulting gladness, and the notes
    Of glorious prophecy.

Now low-voiced as the humming-bird, or bee,
    Or delicate fluttering

Of fresh-blown rose-leaves, when the south wind stirs
    Them with his drowsy wing.

Deepening to holier strains, until the air
    Reeled, with its awful grandeur overcome,
Like rare church music blown through stops antique
    Under a minster dome.

Then all at once the faint flowers raised their heads,
    A light air stirred the palms;
The birds rejoiced, and Nature's self upraised
    Her voice in solemn psalms.

II.

I SAW a poet, sitting in the dusk,
    Clothed in eternal youth,
With low-tuned harmonies and wistful eyes,
    Waiting the dawn of Truth.

Pale as the statue, patiently he sate,
 Watching the clouds unfold,
Thrilling with eager response, as the light,
 Feeble at first, grew bold.

Welcoming with tender melodies each thought,
 His duty to translate;
His lot to bear the chilly herald dews,
 Alone to watch and wait.

But when the gates of morn were open flung,
 And heaven flashed on the sight,
His was the glorious privilege to greet
 With joy and song the light.

Upon his brow gleamed bright its earliest ray,
 And round his temples broad,
Like that which haloed Moses when he walked
 Fresh from the voice of God.

Then were his lips filled with unconscious lays,
 Interpreting all strange

7

And hidden things that are, of love and life,
    Eternity and change.

And by some marvellous influence the proud
    Grew gentle at his song;
Hope brightened o'er the patient, and the weak
    Took courage, and were strong.

SONNET.

HAVE you forgotten the blest eve we sate,
   Awed by the tremulous murmur of the leaves,
   Rustling above us from low beechen eaves?
You twining violets, with calm eyes, as Fate
Serenely weaves our woof predestinate.
   Dear flowers, the symbols of my future years—
   All my heart's impulses, its hopes and fears,
Heaved through my broken utterance. As the weight
Of fresh fallen rain-drops bends some gentle flower,
   Thus drooped your fair cheek toward me with its
      tears,
   When (like a dream the Memory appears)
I dared to kiss you.   In a purple shower
   Neglected fell the violets.   How bright
   Seemed the red sunset, and the moon that night!